The THREE DAYS OF THE LION

The THREE DAYS OF THE LION

JOSE M. MARTINEZ

Cover design by Bill Francis Peralta
Interior design by Jomar Ouano

Published in the United States of America

ISBN: 978-1-68270-763-0
Fiction / Religious
16.03.09

If you thought the Son was dead, think again.

—Jose Martin Martinez

CONTENTS

O death, I will be thy death;
O hell, I will be thy bite.

—Hosea 13:14

PREFACE

For God so loved the world that He gave His one
and only Son, that whoever believes in Him shall
not perish but have eternal life.

—John 3:16 (NIV)

One Sunday in June of 2014, I was sitting in church, listening to our pastor speaking in descriptive terms regarding the death of Jesus and how He rose on the third day. To my bewilderment, those simple words, which I had heard hundreds of times before, began and continued to swirl around in my head for days. On July 1, 2014, those and other words were echoing so loud within my mind that I felt I had to write them down, hoping to catch any measure of relief from the incessant impressions.

This book is a reflection of those thoughts.

By no means am I a biblical scholar, a pastor, priest, preacher, rabbi, any type of self-proclaimed prophet or a scholastic student of the church. However, in my heart and mind, I have come to *feel* that Christ is very much a reality as well as His Angels, which abound about us in incalculable numbers. And, just to clear the table, I have not had any visions, nor am I dying.

As I was typing these words, I found that they came freely, easily, and surprisingly, without great preponderance. This was a very unusual development, because I soon realized that what I was writing was, in my opinion, pure speculation and nearly all the events depicted in this book had no technical source of origin. It dawned on me to begin to research some of the details included in this story, and to my astonishment, I found very little in the Bible to support the basis for the words in this story. Different chapters and verses within the Bible describe in vague and limited terms that Jesus died and rose again in three days, and that is just about the length and breadth of the most monumental event in the history of humanity.

The words in *The Three Days of the Lion* are not based on what I think actually happened, because I do not know what happened, but rather describe what *may* have happened between the time Jesus's physical body died and when His divine spirit ascended into heaven.

A very unnerving development occurred during the course of writing the chapter Day Two. This segment reflected names; hierarchies; and natures of Lucifer, his legions of demons, as well as to what constitutes Hell. I turned to online Christian sources in order to research and substantiate legitimacy with the stunning words I had written. I became uncomfortably nervous while learning about these evil sources, their tendencies, and what they likely represented. I had a horrifying read about what contrived the dark side of the universe. This negative and destructive knowledge unexpectedly caused dark thoughts to also swirl around in my consciousness.

These thoughts soon made it difficult for me to just think straight, to focus on my job and my family. I had to continually concentrate tremendously just to function rationally during the everyday events of my employment, and several times, I found myself getting up out of my work seat just to walk for a few seconds and try to clear my head.

Contrastingly, when my work on Day Three began, I began to feel more relaxed and actually comforted because of the uplifting and inspirational nature of this chapter, in which, as the chapter tries to sincerely describe *how* life might have triumphed over death, I honestly felt that my Father in Heaven was with me all along and that He helped me to tread carefully back into the *light*. The dark thoughts began to fade away.

Amazingly, the words in my head had flowed outward so quickly and easily that I finished the raw first draft in two weeks and a decent revision within about two more weeks! When I sat down to read the revision, I was astonished with the words, particularly because I had never before undertaken any serious consideration about the three days after Jesus's death. To my relief, as I was finishing the revision, the thoughts in my head began to finally quiet and soon stopped.

In retrospect, I must admit that I do not understand how individuals can openly and solemnly give up their beautiful and wondrous minds and spirits over to negative and destructive behaviors including antimoral and unethical habits, as well as tendencies such as lying, cheating, stealing, killing, and conducting profane ceremonies, to name a few. Then again, I have certainly sinned in my life and could never cast any stones.

What is very saddening is why some in America—a country founded on religious principles— not only insist on removing God forever from public sight but try every day to turn those persons away from their own deeply felt, positive, caring, and loving considerations for God.

Well, that being said, I promised a short story, and before my preface gets too long, it is my sincere wish that you have a pleasant and enjoyable experience reading *The Three Days of the Lion.*

Que Dios los bendiga. May God bless you.
Jose Martin Martinez

And one of the elders saith unto me, weep not: behold the lion of the tribe of Judah, the root of David, hath prevailed to open the book, and to loose the seven seals thereof. (Rev. 5:5)

PROLOGUE

The Lord is close to the brokenhearted;
He rescues those whose spirits are crushed.

—Psalm 34:18

He knew these were His last moments. His whole life was endured for just this day. Even as He hung there on the man-made tree in the last moments of His life, helpless, in indescribable pain and suffering, Jesus could no longer speak.

His arms, both dislocated from His shoulders, caused His whole upper torso to feel as if it were on fire as it seared in untold agony. The deep gash, where the Roman soldier pierced His side with the pointed edge of a battle spear, bled with what little remaining blood still coursed through His ravaged body. Both of His hands and both feet were punctured, ripped through by gigantic nails as they were hammered through His bones and into the wooden boards on which He now hung.

Even now, the movement of His heart was slowing, and the strength of His breathing was so very labored. He had no more stamina to even gasp for air…no power to even move His lips. Yet, in this living horror, in His last few seconds, even as He freely forgave the barbaric soldiers who had committed these mindless atrocities upon Him, final thoughts and questions continued to filter through His mind:

Why? Why have you forsaken Me? This pain is too…Oh! Father! You never told Me it would be so much…so…so much! Why? I feel so empty…I have given You everything, My cup is empty. Why? Did I not do as You asked? Did I leave something undone? What have I done to make You so angry at Me? Help Me, Father. I am…I am filled with hurt and sorrow. My life is slipping away, but is My work truly finished? The end of My life is near, and You seem so far away. Everything seems so far away…Help me, Father. I only want to be with You…Take Me…to You, My Father…Please, Take me to You…take Me… My heart…Father…I…love…

His final breath was filled with burning anguish, and then He exhaled for the last time. It was over. He hung there in His last moments, alone, as the onlookers laughed, scoffed, and spat upon Him, ridiculing Him…even in His death.

Only His family wept for Him.

The mocking laughter was deafening. The Roman soldiers and attending Pharisees had had quite an eventful and memorable day, putting this lowly, upstart Carpenter to a miserable and pain-filled death. They ridiculed and jeered this ragtag of a man all day long and saw to their satisfaction that His torment and death would serve as a sterling example for all who might dare follow in His insubordinate and blasphemous ways.

Now He was at peace. His desolation and affliction had finally come to an end. The spectacle was over.

Now He was gone.

DAY ONE

And God said, "Let there be light."
And there was light.

—Genesis 2:1

"You...You? What?" the Fallen Carpenter asked himself. "I am thinking. How is that so? Has not the end come? Am I not at My end? How is it I am here? Where is this place?"

Thoughts were now sifting through His mind as awareness gradually returned. "My mind is so...empty. I feel so...so heavy and yet so empty. How? Why? What is this place?"

Everything was pitch-black. Was this darkness only in His mind? It was as if all life was gone and there was no life left to live or see. "I feel so weak and tired," Jesus murmured to Himself. "There is no strength to open My eyes. Is it as it should be?" Lingering doubts still swirled within His mind.

He subconsciously moved His left hand to His face to rub His eyes and felt the sensation of touch upon His…His forehead? "What? How is it I can feel My hand touching My face? Why is there a feeling as I place My hand upon my face?"

He caressed His face slowly, gently, then moved His hand carefully again toward His eyes. Again, He felt the impression of His fingers, first on His eyebrow, and then slowly, He lowered them toward His eyelids. He immediately grimaced when He felt sensation again, this time against His left eye, suddenly realizing that His eyes were open.

Both were wide open.

"What is this dark place? How is it there is no light?" he asked Himself. Unnerving… empty darkness, all around… no noise, no color, no…no sign of any sound or movement, just black emptiness. Then He began to remember. His life…His joys, His sorrows, and…the… unimaginable, endless pain. The anguish was still fresh in His mind.

"No! No! Never again! No!" he told Himself.

He did not want to relive such atrocious horrors ever again. After all, no man but He had neither ever experienced the greatest torment ever imagined nor endured such sorrow as He did, or even prayed as much as He did. All the while, during His end moments, He had felt as if His Father seemingly forsook Him, forgot Him, even as He felt the increasing weight of all humanity's failings falling endlessly, mercilessly upon His shoulders and His soul.

He had prayed all of His life to the Father, and in His last moments, it felt as if His faithful prayers went unheard. Horrific, incalculable pain had brought lingering doubt.

Then again…Jesus was here, wherever "here" was. And He was…alive? No, His body was not alive. His life force had certainly ended, but His mind very much was…aware? "And…the pain? Where…where is…the…the unending pain? It is…no more? How is this so?" He asked.

The pain was very much gone. And so, in that respect, prayers were indeed answered.

And…how is it I can sense My thoughts? He wondered. *Did I not end as My Father told Me I would? Did I not breathe My last breath on that… that…heinous tree? Did I not feel My life slipping from Me as I grew weaker with each passing moment?* So many thoughts…so many questions. After all, He was only human. He was only…was…a man. A… mortal man. A ghost? What was He now? Where was He? And where is the light?

I am confused. I cannot see, yet I can think. He reasoned as logic began to filter further back into His mind. Even in these moments of darkness, He knew who to pray to. "Light! My Father! Please! I must have light!" He cried out into the darkness.

And there was light.

The light was immediate and excruciatingly brilliant. It was so blinding that He momentarily could not see. It was so…all consuming. He winced as He covered His eyes with His hands to shield His blurred vision from this overpowering onslaught of…blue? Blue light? The…blue… was all around Him…above, to His sides, everywhere. *First darkness, now…now light is all around Me?* He wondered.

"I prayed for light, and the light came. Am I at last in My Father's house? Where are You, My Father?" He asked himself.

And a voice answered to Him, "Your Father awaits you, my Lord."

Slowly, his vision cleared and could soon see the blurry but bright silhouette of a very tall, powerfully framed, and heavily armored soldier standing before him—his silver armor and harnessed sword glistening brightly in the light—bowing before the Son. The Soldier, who stood about nine feet tall and had long, thick platinum hair falling from his shoulders, stood upright and told Jesus, "It is as it should be. You now dwell in the house of the Father, and You will soon sit at the right hand of your Father. Blessed is the Lamb! He carries the sins of the world!"

From all directions, an earsplitting, thundering chorus of voices echoed, "Glory be to the Father and to the Son!"

The Soldier then motioned to Jesus to stand but did not reach out to Him to help him rise. The Son of Man was… down…on His hands and knees? Yes, the Son had been kneeling down all this time. When Jesus was finally able to stand up under His own power, He looked at the…the garb He was wearing.

It was the same loin cloth He wore in His last mortal minutes, but it…it was completely clean and cleared of any sign of His earthly flesh and blood. The Armed One motioned again for Jesus to follow him down a golden brick-laden path leading toward an even brighter and more blinding light off in the far distance. The Lamb carefully took a few measured steps, groggily at first, then took a few more steps along the golden walkway. "I am Michael," said the Armed One. "I serve the Lord, and I serve You. Come, We journey to the great hall of Your Father."

First greeted by darkness, then by all-consuming, sky-blue light…and now I will finally join with My Father, the Lord of Hosts, Jesus thought as He followed Michael. *It is just. It is as it was written. I am weak, but My pain has passed, and I am home at last, with My heavenly Father.*

"Why is everything blue?" Jesus asked the Soldier.

The Great Warrior responded, "It is the hue of faith, my Lord."

Jesus moved forward with small steps. He felt that His walk was still very strained, which was quite understandable, given such immeasurable affliction. But He also began to sense feelings of great joy and warmth as they filled His soul and…spirit? As His vision continued to clear, more colors began to greet His eyes. So…so many colors. He gasped in astonishment as He gazed upon colors He…He had never…seen before. Soon, as His strength of essence grew, He began to make out silhouettes of voluminous rows of assemblies standing at either side of Himself and the powerfully framed Archangel—multitudes of endless faces…all smiling and chanting passages of eternal glory, love, and praise. As Jesus passed, they all bowed in homage.

Beautiful four-winged Cherubim next appeared, filling the openness above this…this place, flying above and swirling about to get within view and to glance upon the Prince of the Universe, of the Lamb, Who was finally home.

As Jesus and the Warrior continued down the golden lane, the Lamb soon beheld the presence of Powers, warrior Angels tasked with doing battle against the forces of darkness in defense of humanity and the Universe. They too bowed in humility before…the Son of Man.

Soon, the light within the great cavern became even brighter and more intense. But the body and eyes of the Son were quickly gaining strength and were now adjusting easily to the great brilliance. It was then that Jesus realized that while His body's strength was returning; so was the strength of His mind. His walk was now not as strained, his breathing—not quite as labored. Something…curious was happening to His essence.

Indeed, subtly, more of His prayers were being answered. After all, had He not just died?

The Warrior paused momentarily, glanced backward at Jesus, as if in surprise, then turned again and continued on the trek. *Odd,* Jesus thought. *What would cause the Great Soldier to pause, particularly here at home?*

To His delight, the realization soon filtered into His mind that He could hear clearly.

However, just as astonishing, He realized that when the Soldier spoke, his lips did not move. Then, again, Jesus's lips also did not move when He spoke. It was as if…as if spoken words were unnecessary and that Their thoughts alone carried Their words. They could hear each other's minds speaking.

To His delight, He could make out the sounds of singing rising in the distance. Soon He could make out the words of the songs of praises bellowing out of the minds of what seemed like thousands of Seraphim, the oldest and highest order of Angels, each radiating with the light of a star and clothed in what appeared to be white fire. Then He beheld youthful Cherubim who could be heard speaking—also with their minds—nonstop.

Jesus wondered why the young Cherubs were not carrying YHWH.

As Jesus and Michael approached the massive host of lecturing Cherubim, the words and singing paused, and all became silent. Looming large before the Son and the Warrior were titanic, blinding-silver-colored doors, which began to open before Them.

Excitement grew within the Son. He would soon see His Father. The Visitors stepped into a monumental room with silver walls, which seemed to reach up to the stars. Stars! Yes! So many glittering stars! The Son could see far up into the very sky!

Once inside the great hall, the doors closed behind the Visitors and came together with a great thud. They continued down the golden path, and soon the singing began again.

Dominions, the Angels of leadership, next came within view, standing tall and staring fearlessly at the two Visitors made their way past them. They too were speaking endlessly, their voices carrying as numerous echoes within the Great Chamber. This order of Angels also bowed down before the Prince of Peace and His guide.

Next appeared the mighty Virtues, keepers of the order of nature in the Universe and of Heaven. Virtues worked hand in hand with the Dominions to keep order in all of God's celestial realities.

Principalities, multidimensional carriers of the words of the Dominions, next appeared, dressed in brilliant metallic armor not unlike that of the Great Warrior. Actually, they were appearing and…disappearing…and appearing yet again. It was as if they were going in and out of this and other realities.

Throughout Their journey, They saw great numbers of Angels and Archangels hovering above Jesus and the Soldier, fluttering about with great excitement, clasping their hands, and smiling with great joy at the Great One, the Prophet, the Bread of Life, Who carried the sins of the world. Even while hovering aloft in the sky, the endless count of God's messengers lowered their heads in homage to the Prince of Peace. For was He not the Christ?

Michael suddenly stopped walking and stood motionless, staring up into the sky for many moments. Then he unsheathed his sword and raised it high into the heavenly sky. This mystical gesture summoned the Archangels Uriel, Rafael, and Gabriel. All three arrived, garbed in mesmerizing gold-and-white frocks, hoisting golden trumpets; and while hovering above the heads of the Great Warrior and the Morning Star, they raised the horns to their lips and blew with great power and duration, filling the sky with one high-pitched note, seemingly for several minutes. Then the trumpeting halted, the noise faded, and soon all began to fall silent.

All chanting ceased, all singing ended, and there was great silence throughout the great hall. Moments later, in the distance, the Divine Son made out a massive golden silhouette of a mountainous figure moving toward Him and the gathered assembly. Soon, the Son could see a great entourage of millions and millions of small-winged cherubs carrying a great figure upon their shoulders. Soon, four very large and radiantly garbed Cherubim draped in white robes appeared, heralding the arrival of the Alpha and Omega.

The Great Transport soon stopped and hovered in the air, not perhaps a thousand yards before the Lamb and the Soldier. Then a great and deep voice was heard. It resonated throughout the great hall but was kind, caring, and gentle in tone.

"My Son, my Light and my Heart! Blessed is my Son, for He did not forsake my word! Blessed is my Most Holy Son, who took the sins of the world as His burden! Behold my Firstborn and the Just One!"

The ensuing chorus of praise was so deafening and powerful that it moved the garbs covering all the hierarchies of Angels, as well as those of the Son's and the Great Warrior's. Even though the strength of the Lion of the Tribe of Judah was gradually returning, this sudden exultation and proclamation of His arrival clearly humbled Him, moving the Son to weep. Tears flowed freely from His eyes, and great joy filled His heart. He raised His hands to wipe the flowing rivers from His face.

And it was then that He saw the holes in both of His palms.

The stunning sight startled Jesus, but they reminded Him of who He was and why He was here. The clarity of the mind of the Son was now…suddenly…suddenly strengthening with an ever-accelerating velocity and was now strong and clear. It was then that the Son of Man—the Morning Light, the Lion of the Tribe of Judah—remembered. He remembered it all.

There was no longer any doubt in His mind about Himself, His Father, or of what was now transpiring at this time in this place. For while His strength was returning, His understanding of the here and now, His presence of mind, had fully returned. While He clearly remembered the horrific affliction of recent days and why He endured it, He now also clearly recognized *this* place for what it was not: this was not His Father's house.

He understood now in His still-tortured heart and soul what was occurring and recognized that this overt and false adulation and praise was exactly as it should be, because it was foretold to Him by His Father.

Then there was that odd reaction by Michael earlier, when the Soldier turned briefly at the Lamb, seemingly startled or surprised. Why would the Light of the World give pause to the premiere and most faithful Soldier-at-Arms? Jesus now understood why: Michael had sensed that immeasurable and limitless power within the Son was multiplying at a stunning and rapid pace. He could now consciously feel forces building within His astral frame. Yes…something curious, indeed, was happening to His essence.

Yes, Jesus also clearly understood where He was, why He was brought here, what was transpiring, and what was about to take place. His earthly pain and limitless suffering had indeed just ended, but the earthly torment He had just endured would seem as nothing compared to the Great Spiritual Ascension of which was already commencing. But the Son further understood that His heavenly spirit was being purged to make way for limitless and godly immortality.

The full wisdom, knowledge, and power of the Father now pouring into Him felt like an all-consuming, titanic wave. Into the soul, mind, and astral spirit of the Son did the manifestation of the escalating force of the Trinity proliferate, and He began to gasp at the enormity and searing supernatural pain of the full and complete heavenly power of the Father. It felt like His soul-force was being ripped vigorously apart at the cellular level. And yet the Host remained fully intact.

"Father," Jesus prayed, "this is…so…so far beyond the anguish I felt at the tree! Fill Me with Thine unending strength!"

In immediate answer to His prayer, the glorious gift of eternal invulnerability set in, and the pain began to ebb. Also rising within and wracking the formerly mortal mind of the Son was the All-Knowledge, and He now gasped as He was instantly able to visualize and comprehend all of God's astonishing plans from the endless past, present, and far into the infinite future.

Indeed, the Ascension was honing His powers of perception at infinitely accelerated levels, and Jesus soon began to see through the false visage of the powerful Armored One. The Great Soldier, Jesus could now see, was not Michael.

Indeed, the Faithful and True One also now realized that not only was He not in the house of His Father, but that the mists veiling the gathered hosts were also fading, revealing that the assembled masses were not the blessed Nine Orders of the heavenly cosmos.

Jesus was in the house of an ancient one He had met before, not so long ago.

The Lamb stood in the house…of the Great Deceiver.

DAY TWO

Be strong and courageous, do not be afraid
and tremble at them, for the Lord your God
is the one who goes with you. He will not
fail you or forsake you.

—Deuteronomy 31:6

All this time, Jesus was deceived into believing this was the House of Heaven, when in fact, it was the House of the Fallen One.

The Voice spoke again:

"Thy Great Tribulation, Thy grief and woe is passed, my Son. Be now soothed. Rest Thee now with Thine Father. Let Thy spirit be abundant and know I am always with Thee. Be not troubled, my Son." The Voice then paused.

Jesus stood silent, without response. He could barely mask the subtle grimace on His face. The Heavenly Ascendancy continued to fill Him with ever-increasing velocity and intensity. With each passing instant, the strength and breadth of the Holy Spirit and the knowledge of His mind multiplied to never-before-imagined levels and did neither stop nor diminish. He knew that the Great Time was here and welcomed it with an open mind and soul…with great compassion…with great faith and confidence. His essence, initially wracked to its core from the onrush of the full force of the Trinity, grew exponentially in celestial fortitude even as His agonized mettle eased.

He was surely well-prepared by the Alpha and Omega. Indeed, it was the Time of the Great Transformation.

But the Great Deceiver also knew what was transpiring, for was it not written? The Dark One had always known that the Great Ascendancy would begin in Hell. And while the immortal soul of Jesus continued to transform geometrically into the holiest and most powerful of all multidimensional spirits, the Father of Lies was cognizant that the glory before Him could not be halted because it was written as such throughout all the celestial realities by the Hand of the Most High.

Nevertheless, the King of the Bottomless Pit was himself fully and celestially empowered, having developed formidable and supernatural omnipotence to loathsome levels during eons of evil contrivance and was now very well-prepared…prepared to turn this event into his finest hour of malevolence. He knew what He had to do. And so the Dark One began to spin his greatest web:

"My son. I have always cared for Thee and am, therefore, Thy True Beginning. I was not the Old One who allowed such misery, such humiliation and pain to wrack and overcome Thy mortal shell. Did I not offer Thee all Thy heart could desire? Did I not lay at Thy feet, the futures of all of the limitless dimensions, their lands and their peoples? Did I not present and warn of the truly selfish vanities dwelling deep within the heart of humanity and offered its cleansing for service unto Thee? I did.

"Truly, this is not the blasphemous Heaven dwelled upon by the Oldest One, but it is the House that now welcomes Thee. This is not Thy Heavenly Home, but Thou art truly in Thy rightful home, at long last. It is my word that Thou will never again know shame or agony or loneliness, as Thine earthly shell did on that sorrowful mortal plane. Thou will find shade and water here. Thou will finally find rest, affection, and companionship denied Thee all Thine days, of Thine whole life."

Jesus's perceptive powers continued to increase with geometric velocity. The great winged entourage assembled before Him began to take on clearer definitions and dimensions. From the corners of His eyes, the Morning Star could notice that the mists of deception had finally dissipated in all directions; and the hordes of assemblies gathered on all sides, which had at last taken on discernible silhouettes with ghastly detail, were not the beautiful and brightly lit Angels of the Lord.

They were the horrifying hosts of darkness: the legions of Satan.

Many were winged. Many had multiple limbs, heads, and twisted hairy torsos; and still others were contrived with nightmarish facial features, including gaping mouths with tongues that dragged along the ground as they slowly skulked toward the Light.

The ground…the ground itself and all the areas and sky surrounding the Son were also transmuting, from beautiful and sparkling shades of blue into repulsive and abhorrent colors of crimson red, foul deep greens, and empty pitches of black. Some of the…the blackness now surrounding Him was actually…dripping? Dripping like molten tar from the…walls?

The Soldier was also changing, slowly, almost imperceptibly, but changing. He must have wielded truly awesome power to have hidden his spiritual structure from the Son, who was himself already filled with great perceptive power, even before arriving at this… this place of hideous pestilence.

Oddly, Satan was not transforming. But the Dark One was fully aware that Jesus was transforming. His greatest moment of pride and arrogance was at hand. The King of the Bottomless Pit continued:

"Thou begins to see, to understand, dost Thou not? I presented my mighty one not only to greet Thee upon Thy arrival, but to further assure Thy safe sojourn to me. He will serve Thee as he has me, and from hence is Thy shield and protector. He called himself Michael to allow Thy traumatized mortal mind to gradually strengthen neither with fear nor doubt, but with fellowship and security. Thou hast surely resurrected but only because of my love and care for Thee. Thy true home is here. Behold Thy family! Rejoice! Thou art truly home!"

Each wicked lie uttered by the Dark One allowed the Lamb to be assured of whom He was facing: the Darkest One, the Fallen One, the First and Most Beloved Angel whom His Father had ever created. Jesus could still perceive out the appearance of the Once-Lucifer, and true to the ancient Scriptures, his visage had not changed. He remained not hideous, not repulsive, nor even horrifying to look upon. Indeed, he was breathtaking in his beauty. The Evil One had bright, *golden*, and penetrating eyes; an astonishingly youthful appearance; and long, platinum-shaded locks not unlike that of his Great Warrior. His face was so striking that it glowed with bright, golden light.

It was odd that the Now-Satan was still so beautiful, while the true forms of his unholy hordes were now fully revealed to the mind of Jesus. The power of the King of Darkness must truly be without measure.

And in keeping with the descriptive tones of the Holy Scriptures, the words now spewing forth from the lips of the Great Deceiver were truly comforting and so very... tempting.

Nevertheless, His pronouncements did not have the ring of truth. Indeed, the Light had faced the Abaddon before and knew what to expect and to not fall blindly under the enchanting spell of the most alluring and most perfect of His Father's Lights. The Power also now deciphered that the babbles spouting forth from the Lost One were nothing more than subtle commands to the gathered host of pestilence, nothing more than temptations, nothing more than…lies.

Suddenly, the Beast roared with laughter and began to raise the strength and tone of his voice as he continued with his offers of everlasting pleasures.

"Deceiver? Thou dost cast me as a deceptive shadow when I present to Thee, before all these multitudes gathered here at Thy feet, the truest and finest gifts of the Heavens, of Earth, of man, indeed, of all dimensions of time and existence? Thou—whom I have only ever offered, in the past and even now, the very life of the Universe for Thy bidding—wouldst cast my gifts aside for further misery?

"No, My Son! Thou wouldst be the Master here, not as it would be in the house of the Old One, where Thou wouldst be further tasked with increased labors, burdens, and pains!

"Behold! The hosts are gathered forthright only for Thy glory and art Thine to command! Since time immemorial, all the souls here have fallen prey to temptation, to darkness, to agonizing suffering, to ancient pestilent plagues, and to all by the Hand of the Oldest One! Their misery hath truly been never ending, yet they eagerly answered my call and gathered here to be finally delivered from the Unfair One to dwell with the True One. They stand here, with great inspiration, to serve Thou, and only Thou!

"Behold their infinite number!!"

A deafening wave of approving howls, shrieks, and squeals rose to mind-shaking levels; and even the walls of the great dark hall shook! Tears appeared and began to rain from the faces of the gathered wayward souls and poured from the very skies, as if a great storm had opened its burgeoning belly.

The tears of the untold legions of lost souls fell upon Jesus not unlike screaming pleas for deliverance. The Lamb felt the many tears of not only all those hovering above him but the moisture from all sides as well. The Son began to gasp and appeared as if He would drown in the endless waves of water now engulfing him.

But these false tears of joy were yet another miscalculated move by the Wicked One, another attempt to blindside and coerce the Lamb—a false hope that now utterly failed.

In his shortsighted, selfish vanity, in his unyielding arrogance, the Evil One failed to bring the Son to His knees. He, instead, managed all imprisoned souls to caress the Son by their very tears. As each tear fell and touched upon His arms, shoulders, head, and face, He now knew the life, the name, and the pain of each anguishing soul.

The tears of the lost ones were also having another unexpected effect: they were augmenting the magnitude of the Ascension. Jesus was beginning to approach full and eternal godliness.

In his blind disdain for the Father, Satan's great and arrogant attempt at temptation had inadvertently commenced the fulfillment of the Holy Scriptures by allowing the tears—and souls—of the unforgiven multitudes to caress and further empower the Light and the Life.

As each of the billions upon billions of tears touched the Son, His heavenly glory multiplied a thousandfold. The True Tribulation was now fully underway, and it was all because of the selfish, self-serving nature of the Father of Lies, who was even now fulfilling the magnificent prophecies of the Holy Bible!

At long last, the Son of God called out, with full knowledge and omnipotent spirituality:

"Lucifer! I know thee! Thou art not the Father! Now, behold, Ancient One! I Am the Father, the Son, and the Holy Ghost! I Am *thy* Father! I didst create thee! Thy vanity and pain is My sorrow, but thou can never be the *I Am*! My will can never be Thine, for even now, thou dost spew pleasure, eternal life, and everlasting power in a most foul and filthy measure of manipulation!

"I am here in fulfillment to the Holy Scriptures as My Father commanded so long ago, and now see thee for what thou truly desires! Thy web is confounding to all but the Light, and it is as clear to Me as the forgiving grace of My Father! Thou hast failed yet again, Most Beautiful but Unclean One! Thou wert the First Beloved but art now the Reviled One! Thou dost now bellow before Me as the Satan, the Fallen, the Most Vain and Lost of all phantoms! Thine innate, duplicitous essence has not altered in all these eons! Wilt thou never repent?

"Oh! So lost, blind, and perfidious art thou! The Dragon can never ascend to the Throne! Thine resentment rises as a mad beast in the wilderness that, even now, thou dost fail to control and consumes thee! Woe be to thee, O Fallen One! For Mine eyes and faith are far more eternal than thy base plots!

"How thou dost insidiously and foolishly attempt to crown me as thine son by calling Me so! Thou didst preemptively mask this abyss and its dwellers with sparkling colors and pleasurable tones and melodies, seeking to draw Me into thine eternal web of darkness!

"Woe be now to thee, O Traitorous One! For thou truly knows the calling of My presence here was foretold by the Holy Scriptures and the Judges themselves, and it is a heavenly fire burning and building with great strength within Me! Stand now aside, O Lawless One, for I know thee! Thou hast forever known Me, for I Am that I Am. I Am stands before thee! Behold! I am the Power, the

Light and the Way, and the Truth comes as a thief into your night!"

With each passing moment and with each word that Jesus spoke, the untold number of lost souls and incensed demons grew bewildered, for they did not understand what was about to happen. They were oblivious all along to God's plan, as Satan contrived they would be.

However, the Great Ascendancy occurring now in their Hell was foretold by God and burned into the souls of Satan and Jesus. Even now, the mystical shell shielding Michael from Jesus's powers of perception had finally completely collapsed—revealing a naked, skulking, red and green, long, and black-haired behemoth poised before him. The great-horned and Once-Prince of the Seraphim, Beelzebub, now stood snarling, slobbering, in a menacing stance before the Prince of Light. With great rage and speed, the demon drew his silver sword-turned-brimstone mace and lunged at Jesus, swinging it mightily at the head of the Lamb. But Jesus calmly raised His right hand and froze the soulless one in his stance. The Son calmly called to the stilled specter of sin:

"Beelzebuth? Thou wouldst harm thy Father?"

Jesus lowered His hand, and the repugnant wraith felt himself loosed from the iron grip around his astral presence. Beelzebub then fell upon his knees, weeping, in seeming confusion.

"I ask thee, again. Dost thou seek redemption or everlasting pain?" Jesus asked the slothing ogre.

"I serve Lucifer. He is my brother," the demon whined.

Jesus quickly retorted, "Thy brother Lucifer is lost. Thy stolen soul endures but as an empty, lonely fragment of what it once was. Thy mind is lost. Thou dost tragically serve the Satan. So be it."

The Lion of the Tribe of Judah turned his gaze away from the revolting hulk and now looked upon the gathering in all directions and asked the Great Question, echoing with great volume that could be heard throughout all corners of Hell:

"And so, now, My children, dost thou seek the eternal grace, everlasting peace, and the infinite, forgiving love of thy Father, or whilst thou remain here until the Day of Redemption, the Day of Judgment?"

Upon hearing the loving extension of unconditional forgiveness and salvation by Jesus, Satan became enraged. He stood upright, atop the flotilla of now-loathsome demons, seemingly preparing to charge and attack the Lamb for His pretentious blasphemy in addressing the Accuser's legions. The Father of Lies had indeed, over untold millennia, tempted and succeeded in gathering endless numbers of wayward minds and souls of all those mortals who succumbed to his manipulative temptations of gluttony, lust, greed, wrath, envy, pride, and sloth. In all this time, the Prince of Darkness had grown immensely in dark and festering spiritual power. *This Tribulation, this challenge,* the Dark One thought, *will be this foolish one's last. I was in the beginning, and He holds no sway over me.*

And so the Dragon moved menacingly toward the Morning Star.

When the lost souls and multitudes of demons beheld what was about to commence, shrieks and wails of seismic proportions commenced and thundered about the great chamber, and great fear arose among the gathered hosts. But no sooner had the Serpent of Old began his motion toward the Savior than the Light again calmly raised a hand to the sky, barely over His head, and halted the Son of Perdition motionless, completely frozen, in his tracks, as if a ghostly vise had suddenly closed around him and held him in unbreakable constriction.

The assembly gasped in astonishment at the most awesome display of universal power ever displayed on Earth or in Hell. The Wicked One roared in pain, immediately realizing his helplessness before the vivacity of this former homeless, penniless, and timid Carpenter; and the anguished howls of the Dark One could be heard throughout all the cosmos of God's Universe.

The most awesome and immeasurably dark power in all the celestial dimensions—seemingly infinite since time immemorial, before all of humanity and which commanded the most vile legions of Hell—was held in unbreakable check by the mere raising of the Hand of the True Power.

But Satan was now howling because he also realized that his impudence and brash rage had now unleashed the Great and Unstoppable Purging of Hell. He now writhed in horrific anguish he never felt before in his existence. The pain that he now felt was multiplied by a thousand times, the agony felt by Jesus on the execrable cross. And now something…something was beginning to writhe within the host of the Evil One, and it was making its way from his spectral torso upward to his mouth. The Prince of Lies raised his head to the sky in uncontrollable response to this…this excruciating and imminent eruption. Satan suddenly began to howl in subjected agony…and as He screamed, astral profusions began to spew forth from His mouth!

At first, the ghastly defecations were spectral globs and chunks of phlegm, blood, skin fragments, plasma, and hair; but then Satan began spewing body parts, corpses, animal carcasses, and obscene masses of disfigured demons. The Dark Tempter stood frozen, powerless to move, yet spewed every obscenity he could bellow. The very lips of Satan began to tear at its corners as condemned souls now sought escape from Satan's wretched and infested belly, increasing in volume and velocity as they sought escape.

The False One wailed louder and louder in immeasurable agony as his face contorted outward as his gaping maw was being forcibly pulled apart merely by the Risen Hand of the Light.

When the gathered assemblage beheld the mighty power of God's Hand, they understood their time of redemption and freedom was at long last at hand, and rushed as ocean waves toward the Son, confessing the countless crimes they had committed and tearfully begging in sincere reverence for deliverance from this soulless plight—this cavern of endless darkness, fire, and infernal pain—and to be returned to the Light…to Everlasting Life.

Jesus understood and knew their hardships, for He had been there with them and dwelled in their hearts their whole lives as they sought solace from the darkness. He knew the Father had never left them. Even now, as Jesus heard their cries and prayers for forgiveness and deliverance calling out from the souls of the gathered legions, He felt within His soul their great eternal confusion, loneliness, and sorrow.

Had He not died for them? Jesus had given His life freely, withstanding commensurate agony so that at this proper and given time, commanded by the Lord of Hosts, the Son would at last have the power to deliver them from their strife. As the Hand of Jesus remained held high, unfaltering, the hordes of phantoms streaming from the tearing lips of the Dark One and the spirits and lost souls approaching him from all imaginable directions soon began to transmute in appearance—taking on white, misty, and wraithlike conformations.

But the Raised Hand of the Lamb also effected a secondary command. The ominous cavern was lit up in blinding starlight by the stunning appearance of the Seven Archangels: the True Michael, the True Gabriel, the True Rafael, the True Seroquel, the True Uriel, the True Remiel, and the True Raguel. The magnificently winged warriors hovering overhead within the Great Hall of Torment lowered their heads and raised their glistening arms toward heaven in solemn prayer. Vortices of brilliant white light and whirling winds not unlike God's great pillar of fire called upon by Moses in long-ago Egypt began to appear within the midst of the anguished souls.

In moments, hosts of four-winged Cherubim and Angels began to whisk in and out of the celestial tempests, their radiant white, flowing garbs flickering with golden specks. They reached out toward the saved but weary souls, grabbing and pulling them into the whirlwinds, hoisting them upward and onto their starbright shoulders. The heavenly soldiers, seemingly endless by count, gathered the redeemed souls and subsequently made their way into the dark, blood-drenched sky high above, disappearing into the Lord's celestial dimension.

Redeemed and delivered.

And it was just. For during this great majestic event, the Son had thoroughly and perfectly become the Father.

No more doubts lingered within the Son, no more fears or confusion. He understood that His Father had ordained first a physical purging of his mortal shell in order to take on the sins of all humanity. Here, now, the Spiritual Purging transpired in order to take on the diabolically held sins of all the lost souls in Hell, to cleanse their minds and hearts, and to propel them to everlasting paradise.

The Lamb had come to deliver *all* men and women from their sins, and He did. He came to deliver the souls of recent and long-dead sinners, and He did. He had come to deliver salvation to those who had no opportunities or no recourse in seeking redemption, to those who were unfairly tempted by the Evil One. And He did.

And still the ghostly souls continued to flow from the decrepit, spectral body of the Fallen One. It seemed as if the count of prisoners escaping from within Satan's ghostly carcass would never end. However, in time, the streams of wailing souls began to diminish, and soon, only those who had chosen to remain in Hell of their own volition were left to continue to wallow within the great cavernous chamber inside the aphotic host of the Dark One. Finally, the pain-wracked siphoning of souls ceased, but the Apollyon had paused to rejoice.

"These remaining are mine!" he roared defiantly in delight as ghostly blood and entrails dripped from his mouth. "They choose to remain of their own free will! Thou wilt not have them!"

Jesus, whose loin cloth had vanished and been replaced with a snow-white frock strapped with a light-brown sash around his waist, finally lowered His Hand. Satan felt the unbreakable grip gradually loosen from around his malevolent essence. The Son of Perdition—once glowing with white, pure, brilliant light, with golden eyes and platinum hair, with the purest of snow-white forms—was now reduced to a loathsome and obscenely distorted phantasm, with torn lips and dark-green and red masses of bloodied and rotting ghostly entrails dripping from his shell and with repugnant gases emanating from his guise.

"I can," proclaimed the Morning Star. "But God's patience is infinite. I will come again at the Great Day of Judgment. I will return, as the Scriptures have foretold. But because they have chosen to abide by Thee, I will not ask them again if they wish to seek eternal salvation or to ask them if they wish to continue to remain imprisoned within thine darkly Host of Death.

"I will return to judge them…and thou!

"Satan, thou art not the Father! Thou art not even a son of the Father! Behold! The True Son has become the Father who stands now before thee! *I Am*! *I Am* the Father, the Son, and the Holy Ghost! I am the Alpha and Omega!

"Thou beest the First Angel, My Father's favorite Angel and most highly beloved above all others. But thy incessant posturing and vanity was thine undoing, in the Beginning and even now. Thy past transgressions now come full circle. I have absolved the lost and tortured souls of Hell and now take My leave from this forsaken cradle of torment!

"But before I leave thee, knowest too, O Lost One, O Shameless Prince of Wickedness, that the Father still loves thee and would ask of thee one question. Dost thou wish to repent and receive heavenly salvation from God and deliverance from thy past sins?"

Satan was stunned. Could it be that, even now, after all his past countless transgressions, that the Father still was willing to forgive even *his* eons of trickery, of untold devilry, treachery, and deception? Was it truly possible? His misshapen eyes grew wide with great anticipation and realized that he could actually once again be seated at the Right Hand of his Father in His Heavenly Kingdom. It was an opportunity that the now-ecstatic Lord of Lies, the Fallen One, and the Dark Death was not willing to pass.

DAY THREE

But be ye doers of the word, and not hearers only,
deceiving your own selves.

—James 1:22–27

The Shepherd was offering Satan redemption, forgiveness, and everlasting peace! But before Satan could respond, Jesus suddenly turned to walk away.

"Wait, O Christ!" the Deceiver bellowed, horrified. "Why dost Thou take leave? I have said nothing to offend Thee nor replied to Thine question! I seek forgiveness and eternal redemption. Deliver me from Hell and my transgressions as Thou hast only just offered!"

Jesus turned back around and gazed with full and stern facial contact upon the Great Liar. He knew that Satan would accept the Great Offer of Salvation. But the Christ needed to know Satan's soul. He had read Satan's eyes and his soul and could understand that the Fallen One was sincerely excited about being once again in the Heavenly House of His Father.

But, at long length, He spoke the Great Pronouncement:

"Truly, thou art the Abaddon! Thine words forever persist, laced with false sincerity and abandon. Thou only ponders the pleasures of the present rather than of the eternal. Once again, the vanities burgeoning from thy mind and soul dost betray thee.

"Thou dost seek a place at the Right Hand of the Father when thou cannot even grasp that the Father stands before thee, hearing thy soul and mind. Indeed, thou questions whether the Father would forgive thee when thou knowest that the essence of God is and has always been the unconditional gift of love and forgiveness. Thy thoughts betray thy desire to be positioned at the highest place in My Father's heavenly kingdom, not for the glory of God the Father, but for thine own personal stature, for influence, for selfish gain.

"And most confounding, thou dost not pray to the Father for deliverance with humble sincerity, but arrogantly commands to be delivered from thine own, engendered stench.

"Thine moment was freely gifted, O Most Perfidious One, and instead thou hast spewed yet more falsehoods! And thou didst seek to mask this Hell, thy contemptible minions, and even thy concocted words before the very essence of the Most High! *I Am*! Behold! The Father, the

Son, and the Holy Spirit stand as *one* before Thee! And now, be thee gone, O Deceiver…Thy minions await thee!"

The Firstborn of the Father turned to walk away from the Once-Lucifer.

There now arose a great howl from deep within the stench-filled body of Satan, a great wail unlike anything ever heard since God created Time. The shriek exploded outward into all of God's dimensional realities as the Dark One realized he had failed himself again, as he had done so all those eons ago, in God's Heaven.

This time, Satan had succumbed to his own temptations. In essence, Lucifer had just fallen for the second time.

But the Glory of God had released trillions of pained souls and innocents, held within the confines of the Dark One's Hell for eons, loosed by the gently raised and loving Righteous Hand of God. Those souls and minds were even now making their safe passage upon the infinite shoulders of God's True Angelic Host, to the True House of the Lord of Hosts.

The remaining demon princes bound within the rotting, spiritual carcass of Satan trembled with great fear, knowing well that the Evil One's impending rage and vengeance upon them would seem as unto a thousand Hells.

Even now, the Holiest of Holies was beginning to fade from the view of Satan and his hellish slaves. As He slowly dematerialized, the Savior turned one last time to gaze with sadness at the remaining lost souls. And then the Lamb was gone.

And it was so in that time, during the Three Days of the Lion, that the Holy Ghost celestially empowered Christ. The greatest of all spiritual transfigurations both fulfilled biblical prophesies and manifested the Father's omnipotence within the Son.

Christ yet again triumphed over the False Lion, who did maraud and desolate endless souls throughout the eons with the darkest of evil malevolence. The Three Days, gifted by the Father to the Son, justly increased without measure the celestial glory and power of the Lamb and forever sealed true faith and love for His Father.

And it came to pass that the Father did welcome the Son into His Heavenly Kingdom, into the True Light, created so long ago for this very moment. Jesus had at long last transcended from earthly and hellish torment to infinite and heavenly glory.

The Lamb was now home. The Three Days had come to an end and, for now, would do until the Great Rapture and the Second Coming of the Holy Son of God.

9 780692 973424